Pebble®
Bilingüe/
Bilingual Plus

Máquinas maravillosas/Mighty Machines

Autos de carreras/Stock Cars

por/by Matt Doeden

Traducción/Translation: Dr. Martín Luis Guzmán Ferrer
Editor Consultor/Consulting Editor: Dra. Gail Saunders-Smith

Consultor/Consultant: Betty Carlan, Research Librarian
International Motorsports Hall of Fame
Talladega, Alabama

Capstone press®
Mankato, Minnesota

Pebble Plus is published by Capstone Press,
151 Good Counsel Drive, P.O. Box 669, Mankato, Minnesota 56002.
www.capstonepress.com

Library of Congress Cataloging-in-Publication Data
Doeden, Matt.
[Stock cars. Spanish & English]
Autos de carreras / por Matt Doeden = Stock cars / by Matt Doeden.
p. cm.—(Pebble plus—máquinas maravillosas = Pebble plus—mighty machines)
Includes index.
ISBN-13: 978-0-7368-7642-1 (hardcover : alk. paper)
ISBN-10: 0-7368-7642-1 (hardcover : alk. paper)
1. Stock cars—Juvenile literature. 2. Stock car racing—United States—Juvenile literature. I. Title. II. Title: Stock cars.
TL236.28.D6418 2007
629.228—dc22

2006027793

Summary: Simple text and photographs present stock cars, their parts, and how drivers use stock cars—in both English and Spanish.

Editorial Credits
Amber Bannerman, editor; Katy Kudela, bilingual editor; Eida del Risco, Spanish copy editor; Molly Nei, set designer; Patrick D. Dentinger, book designer; Jo Miller, photo researcher; Scott Thoms, photo editor

Photo Credits
Capstone Press/Karon Dubke, cover, 9, 11, 13; Corbis/New Sport/George Tiedemann, 1, 17; Corbis/New Sport/Sherri Barber, 4–5; Corbis/Ray Grabowski/IconSMI, 14–15; Getty Images Inc./Jonathan Ferrey, 20–21; Ron Kimball Stock/Javier Flores, 6–7; The Sharp Image/Sam Sharpe, 19

Capstone Press thanks Gary Mueller (shown on page 13) of Chisago City, Minnesota, and Team Menard for their assistance with photo shoots for this book.

The publisher does not endorse products whose logos may appear on objects in images in this book.

Note to Parents and Teachers

The Máquinas maravillosas/Mighty Machines set supports national standards related to science, technology, and society. This book describes and illustrates stock cars in both English and Spanish. The images support early readers in understanding the text. The repetition of words and phrases helps early readers learn new words. This book also introduces early readers to subject-specific vocabulary words, which are defined in the Glossary section. Early readers may need assistance to read some words and to use the Table of Contents, Glossary, Internet Sites, and Index sections of the book.

Table of Contents

Tabla de contenidos

Speedy Stock Cars

Zoom!

A stock car races

on a track.

Veloces autos de carreras

¡Zum!

Un auto de carreras corre

en una pista de carreras.

Stock Car Parts

The body gives
a stock car its shape.
Stock cars look a lot
like regular road cars.

Las partes de un auto de carreras

El chasis le da la forma a los autos
de carreras. Estos autos se parecen
mucho a los autos normales que
andan por las calles.

Powerful engines
make stock cars go fast.
They can go twice as fast
as most normal road cars.

Pero estos autos de carreras
tienen unos poderosos motores.
Así pueden correr el doble de
rápido que los autos normales.

Stock car tires
are called slicks.

Slicks help stock cars
grip the racetrack.

Las llantas de los autos de carreras
se llaman llantas pulidas. Las llantas
pulidas les permiten a estos autos
de carreras pegarse a la pista.

Hoosier
Hoosier
Hoosier
RF
QUARTER MASTER
AFCO
TEAMTECH
PENSKE
RACING SHOCKS
Holley
HP CARBS
JERICO
PERFORMANCE PRODUCTS
RACING TRANSMISSIONS
BUTLERBUILT
Professional Seat Systems
Port City
RACECARS
HOWE
Bassett
Motive Gear
MSD
IGNITION
PERFORMANCE
FRICTION
BRAKES
RED LINE
SYNTHETIC OIL
STOCK CAR BODIES
FIVE STAR
RACE CAR BODIES
PERFORMANCE CONCEPTS
CEDAR RAPIDS
ALLSTAR
PERFORMANCE
RACING ELECTRONICS
TORCO
RACING FU
www.torcoracefuels
GM
PERFO
PARTS
HYPER

Seat belts and harnesses
hold the driver in place.
They keep the driver safe.

Los cinturones de seguridad y
los aparejos mantienen al conductor
en su lugar. Así el conductor
está seguro.

harness/aparejo

On the Track

Drivers race stock cars around big oval tracks. Each race lasts hundreds of laps.

En la pista

Los conductores corren en estos autos de carreras alrededor de pistas ovaladas. Cada carrera dura cientos de vueltas.

During a race,
drivers make pit stops.
Pit crews fill the cars
with gasoline.
They also change the tires.

Durante la carrera, el conductor hace
varias paradas en el foso. El equipo
del foso llena el tanque de gasolina.
También cambia las llantas.

Sometimes the drivers crash. The cars can spin, flip, and even catch fire.

Algunas veces los conductores se estrellan. Los coches pueden derrapar, voltearse y hasta incendiarse.

Mighty Stock Cars

The fastest stock car crosses the finish line first.

Stock cars are mighty machines.

Maravillosos autos de carreras

El más veloz de los autos de carreras es el primero en llegar a la meta. Estos autos de carreras son unas máquinas maravillosas.

Glossary

body—the outside frame of a vehicle

engine—a machine that makes the power needed to move something

grip—to grab and not slide around

harness—straps that hold a driver safely inside a stock car

lap—one full trip around a track

pit stop—a break drivers take from the race so the pit crew can add fuel, change tires, and make repairs to a car

slicks—smooth tires that help stock cars grip the track

Glosario

los aparejos—correas que mantienen al conductor seguro dentro del auto de carreras

el chasis—la parte exterior de un vehículo

el foso—lugar donde se detienen los conductores durante la carrera para que el equipo del foso ponga gasolina, cambie las llantas y haga reparaciones al auto

las llantas pulidas—llantas que sirven a los autos de carreras para pegarse a la pista

el motor—máquina que produce la energía para mover algo

pegarse—agarrarse para no derrapar

la vuelta—giro completo alrededor de una pista

Internet Sites

FactHound offers a safe, fun way to find Internet sites related to this book. All of the sites on FactHound have been researched by our staff.

Here's how:

1. Visit www.facthound.com

2. Choose your grade level.

3. Type in this book ID 0736876421 for age-appropriate sites. You may also browse subjects by clicking on letters, or by clicking on pictures and words.

4. Click on the **Fetch It** button.

FactHound will fetch the best sites for you!

Index

Sitios de Internet

FactHound proporciona una manera divertida y segura de encontrar sitios de Internet relacionados con este libro. Nuestro personal ha investigado todos los sitios de FactHound. Es posible que los sitios no estén en español.

Se hace así:

1. Visita www.facthound.com

2. Elige tu grado escolar.

3. Introduce este código especial 0736876421 para ver sitios apropiados según tu edad, o usa una palabra relacionada con este libro para hacer una búsqueda general.

4. Haz clic en el botón **Fetch It**.

¡FactHound buscará los mejores sitios para ti!

índice